To Jane and Rose —K. D.

To Jamie, for always being there to
help with my fairy houses —C. K.

Published by Roaring Brook Press
Roaring Brook Press is a division of Holtzbrinck Publishing Holdings Limited Partnership
120 Broadway, New York, NY 10271 · mackids.com

Our books may be purchased in bulk for promotional, educational, or business use. Please
contact your local bookseller or the Macmillan Corporate and Premium Sales Department at
(800) 221-7945 ext. 5442 or by email at MacmillanSpecialMarkets@macmillan.com.

Library of Congress Control Number 2022920231

First edition, 2023
The illustrations for this book were created digitally, drawn and colored with
Adobe Photoshop using a Wacom Cintiq. This book was edited by Emily Feinberg
and designed by Naomi Silverio. The editorial assistant was Emilia Sowersby. The
production was supervised by John Nora, and the production editors were Hayley O'Brion
and Jennifer Healey. The text was set in Dash Decent, and the display type is hand drawn.
Printed in China by RR Donnelley Asia Printing Solutions Ltd.,
Dongguan City, Guangdong Province

ISBN 978-1-250-79257-0
1 3 5 7 9 10 8 6 4 2

Fiona Builds a Fairy House

WORDS BY
KRISTEN DICKSON

PICTURES BY
CELIA KRAMPIEN

ROARING BROOK PRESS
New York

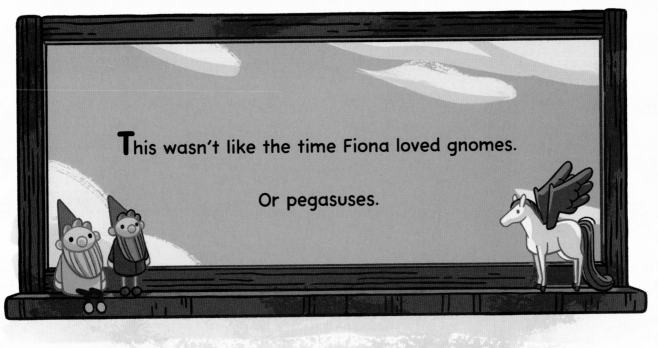

This wasn't like the time Fiona loved gnomes.

Or pegasuses.

Not to mention the unicorns
or the mermaids
or the ogres.

This was definitely different from the ogres.

Because this time, Fiona was into fairies.

It was all she could talk about.

Fairies at breakfast,

fairies at lunch,

fairies at music,

fairies at gym.

"You should build a house
for your fairies," said her teacher.
"Then they'll come visit you."

"A fairy house?" Fiona marveled.
"For my very own fairies?"

This was a game changer.
She got to work recruiting
help right away.

"Can you help me build my fairy house?" Fiona asked her mother.

But her mother had to wash the cat.

"Can you help me build my fairy house?" Fiona asked her father.

But her father had to dry the cat.

Next, Fiona asked her brother.

Her brother had to rescue the cat but then said, "There are no such things as fairies." Which he had also said about the gnomes.

And the pegasuses.

And the unicorns.

And the mermaids.

(He wasn't sure about the ogres. The ogres might be real.)

"I'll show him," said Fiona. So she grabbed her basket, went out to her backyard, and foraged for supplies.

Then she scouted for a location.

By the slide?

No, not near the slide.
Too many running feet.

By the swing?

No, not near the swing.
Too many flying feet.

By the princess castle with
the moat and the dragon?

So Fiona chose the
sycamore tree.

It had great old roots and beautiful bark
and a perfect round hollow.

Fiona unpacked her basket and took inventory. She had . . .

twenty acorns

a ball of twine

some moss

fairy

She drew a blueprint.
She formed a plan.

She gathered everything
she needed to build the
best fairy house ever.

That's when it happened.

A wet cat happened.

A **VERY** wet cat.

All twelve of Fiona's pebbles fell into the hollow of the tree.

Then her mother streaked by,

Her father came next—

Finally, her brother trotted past, just fast enough to upend the ball of twine and the moss.

knocking over all ten twigs.

and so went the twenty acorns.

"Who cares," he said. "I told you fairies aren't real."

Fiona turned to the tree hollow.
Was her brother right about fairies?
Was he right about gnomes?
Pegasuses and unicorns,
mermaids and ogres?

The tree hollow had an answer.

Hello?

"Excuse me, but are you building a fairy house?" asked a gnome as he climbed from the tree.

"I brought one hundred and twelve pebbles with me. Does that help?"

"Yes, thank you," said Fiona. "It's nice to see you again."

The gnome added his pebbles to the basket.
Then another voice called out.

"Excuse me," said a pegasus, flying out of the hollow. "Are you building a fairy house? I brought two hundred and ten twigs with me. Does that help?"

A unicorn leaped out next, with three hundred and twenty acorns.

"Yes, thank you," said Fiona.
"In the basket, please."

Then a mermaid arrived. She brought her own ocean,
along with a net full of twine.

Last came an ogre.

It took him a while to crawl out of the hollow.

But he offered to do the heavy lifting, and his pockets were full of moss.

Fiona took inventory again. Her basket was brimming with supplies, and she had lots of tree-hollow friends to help.

Now did they have everything they needed to build a fairy house?

No. There was still one problem. They had no way to put it all together!

"My boogers are pretty sticky," said the ogre helpfully.

"Or," said Fiona, "maybe the castle has some glue sticks."

So she called down the hollow for the princess, the castle, the dragon, and their moat.

They came right away, but they didn't bring the moat.

Instead, they brought one fairy!

And that one fairy brought one wand, which she used to put the house together.

"Does that help?" asked the fairy. Everyone cheered.

Soon the fairy house was full of friends and joy and crowns and cake.

Fiona even invited her brother. The ogre saved him a seat.